I TURNED MY MOM INTO A UNICORN

TED + FRIENDS

by BRENDA LI

Hardcover:

ISBN-13: 978-1-7752173-6-7

ISBN-10: 1-7752173-6-1

Paperback:

ISBN-13: 978-1-7752173-7-4

ISBN-10: 1-7752173-7-X

Ebook:

ISBN-13: 978-1-7752173-3-6

ISBN-10: 1-7752173-3-7

Published by Summer and Muu

Summer and Muu, Summer and Muu Kids and associated logos are trademarks and/or registered trademarks of Summer and Muu.

Dedicated to my beloved son.

Special thanks to
my husband, my mom and dad,
my sister and her cat.

Once upon a time, there was a giraffe named Ted.

Ted's mom was always mad in the morning.

She was always grumpy in the afternoon.

She was also very grumpy at night.

"Mom is always grumpy,"
Ted thought to himself.

"I wish she would turn into a happy unicorn."
As he wished upon a star, he fell asleep.

The next morning,
a rainbow sparkled across the sky...

Ted went into the kitchen.

His wish came true!

His mom did turn into a unicorn!

Right away, they played together.

BONK!

The unicorn showed Ted
how to make rainbows and gold coins.

It was quite stinky!

They ate their favorite food,

NOM
NOM
NOM

and acted silly together.

BLAH
BLAH
BLAH

Oh no! They even made a mess together!

It was their happiest day ever!

But soon, it was bedtime.

Ted looked at his empty bedroom.
Mommy was not there.

He missed her yummy pancakes,

and missed her at the park.

He missed mommy's bedtime stories,

and missed her bedtime kisses.

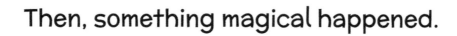

Then, something magical happened.

Mommy came back!!!

Ted jumped with joy!

He gave his mom a big hug and said,

"I'm so sorry mommy! I will never

turn you into a unicorn again!"

Ted put on his pants and picked up his toys.

Mommy gave him a present for being such a good boy.

He opened up the present.

"A UNICORN DOLL!!!!!" he yelled.

He was super happy!

"Thank you mommy,"
Ted whispered.
"I love it, and I love you even more."

Always be thankful for what you have.

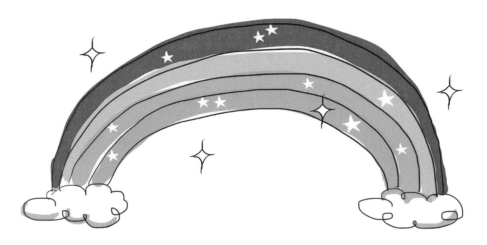

THE END

BONUS LOOK + FIND!

1) How many pizzas are there?
2) How many pink donuts can you find?

1) How many rainbows can you find?

2) How many stars are there?

Made in the USA
Coppell, TX
28 April 2020